W9-BTO-728

Printer's error on pages 89 to 90, but all the text is there
Enjoy the story.
Sharon K Connell

Amethyst Lights

Dedication

Amethyst Lights is dedicated to my Lord Jesus Christ, without whose grace and guidance none of my books would have been written or published.

This story is also dedicated to all those who love grew up reading fairytales.

Acknowledgments

My husband, Arnold C. Hauswald, retired SGM, US Army, for all the late dinners, his support, and encouragement.

The ACFW Scribes Critique Group for their encouragement, advice, suggestions, and encouragement. In particular, Gary Breezeel, Kathy McKinsey, Megan Short, and Lee Russ.

The members of my Facebook Group Forum, Christian Writers & Readers, for their encouragement.

"...be sure your sin will find you out."
Numbers 32:23

Note from the Author

To give the story an old world, Irish feel, I've changed the following words to Gaelic.

Mother to máthair, pronounced ˈmaːhər
Father to athair, pronounced ˈa-hær
Fairy to faery, pronounced the same
Jail to gaol (old world form), pronounced the same as jail
Jailer to gaoler
Jailhouse to gaolhouse

Because of the difficulty of the Gaelic language, and because some words are unrecognizable from the English (as in the case of Fairy/Faery, which in Gaelic is Sióg, among other spellings depending on the type of faery), I have not changed any other words to Gaelic spellings.

Special made-up words for the story:
Shadair: a type of seer with extraordinary powers
Faeryman (men): male fairies
Faerywoman: older female fairy
Faerylet: young unmarried female fairy
Faeryling: baby to child fairy not come of age
Gentlefaeryman: gentleman fairy

All names and made-up words are pronounced phonetically.
I hope these special words are enough to set the atmosphere for the reader.

Enjoy the story.

Amethyst Lights

Sharon K Connell

Chapter One

*L*ylan Chaldre's sight rose from the berries he'd collected off a bush as he hovered near the edge of Emeraldis Pond. Flashing lights across the water attracted his attention. He lowered his feet to the ground.

As his eyes adjusted to the brightness, a village came into view. Where'd that come from? He'd been on this side of Emeraldis many times in his young life when he wandered away from home and their quiet town of Glistineare. He'd never seen this. Why was it glowing with a brilliant purple light? He'd heard no one mention this place. Not that he recalled, anyway.

As he squeezed through the lush growth, he pulled out a twig from his right mint green wing. *Must have picked this up while I searched for Jaden.* Lylan shook his head and spun to rid his thick black hair of any other particles he might have picked up. Debris flew from his forest green tunic.

As he pitched the stick to the ground, Jaden Chaldre burst through the bushes and fell at Lylan's feet. "There you are, big brother. I thought I'd lost y—what is *that*?" Jaden's crystal blue eyes grew as round as the huge blackberries Lylan carried in his sack.

After a hearty laugh at the dried leaves, twigs, and vines that protruded from Jaden's mop of pure white hair, Lylan reached out a hand to help his brother to his feet. One of his powder blue wings had bent in the fall. Lylan straightened his brother's appendage. With his head cocked and one side of his lips hitched, Lylan gazed at Jaden. His younger brother was so excitable. "It's called a village... with a palace."

Focusing back on the amethyst glow over and around what appeared to be a huge castle rising from the center with shanty-type homes surrounding the magnificent structure, Lylan searched his youthful memories. The tales his grandathair Estallan had told him of the town's outskirts were nothing more than made-up stories to him.

In Lylan's mind, he envisioned the elder gentlefaeryman on a toadstool as he told stories to the little ones in their town. His sparkling emerald green eyes, the same color he'd passed down to his older grandson, glistened with excitement as he fabricated adventures for the faerylings. His flyaway white hair, like Jaden's, moved with every gesture, as did his multi-colored wings. *Fabrications. Were they?*

If only Grandathair was still here. Lylan tapped his nose. He and his brother could go to Grandathair's house and ask about this—what? He told Jaden it was a village... but was it? One hundred years ago today, their grandathair had disappeared. Everyone presumed he'd been killed by the raiding party that invaded their town. Was this an enchanted realm that had appeared?

Sharon K Connell

Chapter Two

*L*ady Jillian brushed her waist-length flaxen hair with a vengeance. The Prince of Amythaseah himself had ordered her to attend tonight's gala event in his honor. He was the most irritating faeryman she'd ever met in her long life, despite his royal blood. Coming of age after her eighteen hundredth birthday as a lady noble in the king's court was not all it was hyped up to be, if anyone asked her. Máthair said new responsibilities came with her new status.

"Wear your most becoming gown, dear," her máthair, Lady Vislea, had told her. *"He'll announce the proposal and your upcoming marriage. What an honor this will be! Just think of it. After the prince's coronation, you'll be queen. This cannot happen for another hundred years, according to the laws the shadair laid down. Proposals and marriages cannot be*

performed until the village is released from the curse for seven days every hundred years. I know, dear. This isn't what you wanted, nor I for that matter. But in Maricent's realm, we have to do this to survive. Better to be queen even to him, with a beautiful home, clothes, and food to eat than to grovel in the streets. Isn't it?"

Her máthair rattled on, obviously in an attempt to convince her only daughter. Jillian hadn't answered then. *No.* To marry this prince was *not* better.

Something puzzled her. Jillian laid the brush on her vanity. Why was it their village did not appear to the outside world except for seven days once every hundred years, and then disappear again? What had caused this? Everyone here lived on as normal, but no one in the outer realm could see them. Anyone who came near acted as if nothing was here, except during that one week. Somehow they avoided walking into the gates when the village wasn't seen, which she also didn't understand. They'd veer off in another direction. Yet for those seven days, people from faraway places would visit the royal realm as if it were common place every year.

Jillian pondered. Why hadn't she ever met anyone who resided closer to the village?

Oh, well. She'd never gotten an answer to any of those questions. Not even from the realm's shadair, the old, wise gentlefaeryman who'd lived for more than ten thousand years—so far—and knew everything about everything. *I wonder how long he's counseled the king... and what kind of powers he has.* Whatever they are, he'd only smiled and changed the subject. She giggled.

Jillian stood and gazed at the tall, oval, gold-framed mirror across her bedroom. In the pale amethyst light that filtered through the arched windows, her white gown glowed in shades of pink to magenta. The material sparkled as if strewn with diamond flecks. A thin silver tiara fashioned in the form of a vine with tiny leaves sat on her head and glowed, as did her glittery white wings.

Prince Maricent. The soon-to-be crowned King of Amythaseah. What a bore. *Never cares about anyone but himself.*

She'd battled long and hard with their shadair to avoid this day. What had changed Shadair's mind about allowing the prince to take the throne and call off the search for his athair, missing since the last one-hundred-year break. Along with her athair.

Did she want to be Maricent's wife? He didn't love her. He'd paid no attention to her the few times he'd visited her athair. Stuck on himself, self-centered, egotistical... among other things. The lone reason he wanted to marry her now was because their law said he must wed by his three-thousandth birthday and produce an heir within the following year—*ugh*—to retain the crown. That meant, if he made the announcement of their betrothal tonight, even though she'd never *officially* accepted it, their wedding ceremony would have to take place before the seven days expired.

Maricent wanted to be king of the entire world of Crystandavair. She'd heard him boast of it. A prince could not fully command the royal army. Right now, he controlled a mere handful of guards within their ranks who were loyal to him. But as king, he'd rule. Why did she have to be born a female? Except for her friend, Lady Tallynesa, no other females among the nobility had come of age and remained still unwed.

Poor Tally. She was so sweet, even when others said she wasn't a pretty faery because of her bland coloring. Pale brown eyes, light brown hair, beige wings, and pale skin. Although her eyes were indeed soulful. It'd be fair to say, she'd blend right into the forest during autumn, if it weren't for the colorful clothing she always wore. She reminded Jillian more of the adorable forest pixies than a faerylet. So cute.

Jillian smiled but then bit her bottom lip. If she didn't marry Maricent, he'd choose Tally out of need. Tears came to Jillian's eyes when she thought of the horrible life marriage to him would mean for her friend. Bitterness, ridicule, unfaithfulness, and even abuse. What the prince was known for. *I could handle his abuse.* Dear, gentle Tally would never survive.

Keep telling yourself that, Jillian. Tally was the single friend she had near her age. And the kind faerylet's nature was beautiful. Even Athair once said so.

Athair. He'd never allow this marriage her máthair insisted was inevitable. Why had he left the village to accompany King Farmeran one hundred years ago? Why hadn't he returned in time, before the village disappeared again, and where was Athair now? Where would a king and his counselor from a disappearing realm go when his entire kingdom vanished from view? Had they lost their memories, which was said would be the destiny of anyone outside the realm after the seventh day? She swiped the tears from her cheek. "Oh, Athair. I need you so much right now."

He'd *never* allow his daughter to be sold to a pompous prince. *Athair, will I ever see you again?*

"Dear?" Her máthair called from down the hallway. "Are you ready?"

No. She couldn't go through with this. She'd leave word for Tally to run away too. They had no other choice.

Jillian locked the door to her chamber and leaned back against the polished wood. All her life, she'd dreamed of falling in love with a handsome young faeryman who'd sweep her off her feet. She didn't care whether he was a prince or the son of a lowly merchant. They'd wed and live a life of contentment and companionship. Something she'd never find with Maricent. Sure, he was handsome enough with his hazel eyes and canary-yellow hair that matched his wings. Of course... he knew it too. Chiseled features and muscular build, which the lower-class faerylets swooned over.

No, I won't.

Máthair's almost here. What can I do?

Sharon K Connell

Chapter Three

ith their load of berries, mushrooms, and nuts, Lylan and Jaden flitted their way back to the campsite they'd set up between home and the pond. Jaden's stomach let out a low growl. Lylan chuckled to himself.

"I'm starved, Lylan. Let's eat before I pass out."

"You're always going to faint from hunger, Jaden. All you think about is your stomach."

"Well, unlike you, Lylan, well into your two-thousand, seven-hundred seventy-seventh year, I've not quite become of age yet, only being one-thousand, eight hundred ninety-two years old. I still have a hundred and eight years to go to get to two-thousand. I'm still a growing faeryman." Jaden grinned at his brother.

"Yeah. You'll grow sideways if you don't learn to curb your appetite. What will you do then? Just how much weight do you imagine those wings will carry?" Lylan let out a hearty laugh and lowered the makeshift leaf sack to a rock next to the campfire ring. "Okay, let's eat and make our way home. Athair said we shouldn't be out past twilight tonight, which draws near."

Athair hadn't worried like this about them staying out late for many years now. What was Athair afraid of this night? Lylan munched on his food. Could it have something to do with the old stranger who'd shown up on their doorstep this day a century ago? The poor faeryman looked like he'd been beaten and left in the bushes to die. Over the years, he'd never recalled what happened to him. He didn't even remember who he was or where he'd come from.

Lylan clamped his lips together between his teeth. He'd have to ask his athair what he knew about the fair-haired stranger they'd decided to call Fyan. Had he ever mentioned this strange village with the purple glow? Maybe Athair anticipated another raid on the village like the one a hundred years ago.

As twilight began to fall and the young faerymen finished their meal, the dense trees rustled behind them. Lylan grabbed his brother, placed a hand over Jaden's mouth, and dragged him back into a clump of brush. "Hush. We've tarried too long. It's almost dark, and you know what Athair said."

Jaden nodded.

The bushes parted, and a beautiful faerylet fell out the way Jaden had that afternoon. Her lovely sparkling, white gown appeared to have gone through quite the journey, torn almost to shreds. Her glowing hair, white with a trace of golden hue, flew around her head as if she'd been in a whirlwind. Lylan's eyes narrowed. Who was she? And why was she out so late by herself... with no shoes? She wasn't from Glistineare.

He let loose of his brother, allowing him to fall into the leaves, and stepped out of the shrubs.

Chapter Four

*J*illian almost jumped out of her skin as two faerymen appeared and gazed down where she'd fallen. Her heart raced as she tried to focus on their faces in the increasing darkness. Butterflies swarmed as if they were bees in her stomach. They weren't Maricent's men. She let go of the breath she'd held. Her voice abandoned her. Her heart continued to pound like a hammer against her ribs. She was so tired. Her feet ached. Why hadn't she gone around the swampy part of the pond? She wouldn't have lost her shoes.

A hand stretched forward and grasped her upper arm. The faeryman held out his other hand toward her. She took his hand,

and he lifted her from the ground. "Are you okay?" His voice was as deep as the green of his emerald eyes. Comfortingly mellow. Like Athair's.

"My name is Lylan. This is my brother, Jaden. Can we help you?" He swung his head to indicate the white-haired faeryman behind him. "You look as if you've been in a struggle. Are you hurt?"

Jillian shook her head. "Not really," she squeaked. "Just very tired, and my feet are sore."

The dark-haired faeryman glanced at the ground. "They're bleeding. We need to attend to them right away. What happened to your shoes?" He scooped her into his arms and rushed into the woods with his brother on his heels.

"*No. Please.* I *must* get away." The surrounding air closed in. She couldn't breathe. Sparkles swam in her vision. "*Please,* help me. I'm La..."

Chapter Five

The lantern in the window of their home showed through the last part of the forest as Lylan and Jaden neared the house. They'd face a strong, and long, lecture from their athair once they got home. Lylan held the faerylet close to his chest as he ran. She'd fainted, probably from fatigue. He hoped. Her feet needed to be cleaned and treated. Why would such a beauty be out there alone? Who was she running from?

Jaden sprinted ahead and opened the front door. As Lylan burst into the room, his máthair, athair, and two sisters' eyes flashed toward him.

His máthair threw aside her sewing, flew from the rocking chair, and rushed to him. "Who is this?" Her turquoise blue eyes widened. "What happened to her? Take her to your sisters' room."

Lylan kept up with his máthair's fluttering silver-blue wings without a word. Her platinum-gold hair trailed behind her like a bridal veil. Máthair would take care of her. As the town healer, she always knew what to do.

Their athair followed close behind with his daughters and Jaden. He grabbed Jaden's shoulder as they neared the bedroom but continued to shadow Lylan. "We'll talk later about you two being out so late after my warning. Tell us who this faerylet you've brought home is? And how did she wind up in this condition?"

"Sorry, Athair. We have no answers. She appeared while we were getting ready to head home. Fell on the ground. When Lylan saw how cut up her feet were, he picked her up, and we took off for home. She fainted right after he said we needed to find help for her. She said she *needed* to get away."

His athair furrowed his brow. His face grew almost as dark as his auburn hair and wings. Jaden and their two sisters waited with their athair outside the bedroom doorway as Lylan lowered the faerylet to one of the beds.

His máthair lifted the stranger's right foot and shook her head. "Son, bring a basin of warm water and some washcloths and towels for me."

Lylan rose from his kneeling position next to the bed. Jaden rushed in and touched his shoulder. "You stay. I'll gather everything for Máthair." He strode from the room. His sister Daleah followed him. Lylan turned back to his máthair.

"Now, son. You must know *something*. Who is this faerylet?"

He gazed into his máthair's turquoise eyes. His athair drew near, his chestnut eyes piercing. "Máthair, Athair, I have no idea." He explained what had happened at the campsite.

His athair nodded. "That's what your brother told me."

Lylan pressed his lips tight. "She seemed scared to death. And her clothes were shredded this way, as if someone had chased her in the dense undergrowth of the forest. She must have run through a lot of thickets for her feet and clothing to be in this shape. When she burst through the bushes, she had no shoes on her feet. Do you think she'll be okay?" He glanced down at the beautiful face, which had lost its color and glowed translucent.

Sharon K Connell

Chapter Six

Fedreta smiled at her older son. So... he had feelings for this faerylet. Fedreta's heart warmed. She'd always possessed the ability to perceive what others felt inside, even when they didn't. It had helped in her healing practice many times.

She shifted her gaze to her husband, Toran Chaldre. He had the gift of foreknowledge, which made him head of their faery clan. From his expression, he sensed something now.

Jaden entered the room with a basin of water and towels. Daleah handed a jar of salve to her máthair. "Thank you, dears. You girls ready yourselves to retire for the night. You'll both have to sleep in one bed while I have this faerylet in the other under my care. And I plan to stay with my charge to check on her through the night." Her daughters left.

Lylan glanced at his máthair. "I'll fix up a cot for you." He turned to leave.

"No. You can do it later. I believe you, your brother, and your athair have matters to discuss." Toran should talk to their sons about what troubled him. She'd seen that look before, and it never meant anything good.

Fedreta cleaned the faerylet's feet and applied the salve. She gazed at the sweet face, so pale and still. "What have you gotten yourself into, my dear?" *And how will it affect my family?*

Chapter Seven

Toran sat with his sons in front of the fireplace in the living room. Lylan's eyes drifted toward the hallway which led to the bedrooms. "Son. She'll be fine. Your máthair will see to her needs. Her feet need healing. There's no wound to her heart." As he said the words, his own pinched. Perhaps she was experiencing an emotional problem. He'd have to talk to the faerylet as soon as she awoke. *Someone may be searching for her.* The premonition in his mind was strong. Something was definitely wrong.

"Lylan. Quit staring down the hall and pay attention to me. I want you to go over what happened tonight again. Leave nothing out, no matter how trivial it might seem. I sense... not sure what."

"All right. But do you think the faerylet will be okay? She was so pale."

"Get your mind off her, son. She'll be fine. She's in your máthair's hands." He focused on Lylan. "Go over everything from the time you and Jaden left home this morning."

His younger son's eyes shifted from Lylan to his athair. "The day was going along great. We'd fished in the stream this morning. You know. The one next to the ancient castle ruins. We set up our camp for the day, gathered berries, nuts, and mushrooms. Took a nap. Swam. Then we searched for our evening meal—"

"*Lylan,*" his athair called in his no-nonsense voice. "Staring at the hallway will not help her heal any faster. Look at me, boy." His older son had never been so distracted. "You listen to what Jaden tells me, since he seems to be the spokesman, and make sure he doesn't forget something."

"Yes, Athair."

Jaden continued with an account of his and Lylan's doings, since they left the house in the wee hours of the morning until Jaden said he lost track of Lylan in the woods.

"That's when I came upon Emeraldis Pond at the end of the stream." Lylan's brows pinched together. "As many times as we've visited the fishing hole, I've never seen a glow emanating from across the water. It mesmerized me. I pushed my way through the trees and past the undergrowth to the edge of the pond. And I saw it."

Toran's pulse quickened. He leaned forward. "Saw what?"

Lylan explained what he'd observed, how they'd prepared to go home, and the faerylet's appearance. Toran clenched his teeth. This must be the reason for his premonition. The mystical village. It was back. Could this female be from the cursed realm? He must talk to her. Something bad was about to happen, but he had no idea what it was or how to defend his town and people—his family. But what was it he'd save them from? This wasn't the same sensation he'd gotten a hundred years ago at the time of the attack. The sense of threat was more intense. How could he protect anyone if he couldn't identify the danger?

Chapter Eight

Worry lines spread across the forehead of Lylan's athair. Was Athair concerned the faerylet would die? Lylan's heart ached. She couldn't... not now that he'd found her. What was he saying? He didn't know her. What was wrong with him? Why these weird feelings?

"Athair, do you think the female came from the village at Emeraldis Pond? I still don't understand why it appeared. Has anyone ever been there? Were you aware of it?"

With his lips pressed together, his athair's eyes ping-ponged to Jaden and back. "It's time I tell you boys the history of Glistineare and Amythaseah. From long before I was born almost six thousand years ago."

Before his athair was born? Lylan's breath caught with the idea. He'd overheard rumors from older residents in town. They always stopped talking when younger fairies came near.

"About Glorianderis?" Lylan and Jaden said in unison.

While Jaden sucked in his lower lip, Lylan added, "When Glistineare and Amythaseah were one city?"

Their athair's brows rose. "Yes. So you've heard that much. I'm sure Amythaseah is the village you say you found across Emeraldis Pond. I'm certain of it."

The young faerymen glanced at each other. Questions exploded in Lylan's mind. "Has the village been there all this time and I've not noticed it? Why haven't we come upon it in the past? Something isn't right here."

"Exactly, my son. Something's been amiss with that place for ages. For at least eight thousand years."

This had to be why Athair cautioned them not to stay out past twilight tonight. "You knew the village was there, didn't you?"

His athair nodded. "You see, we were warned—"

"Wait." Jaden lifted his hand in the air. "Are you saying this is an enchanted village?"

"More like a cursed village, son." His athair shook his head and frowned.

Lylan latched onto Jaden's shoulder as the younger faeryman drifted upward from his seat. "Let Athair tell us instead of asking questions and you getting yourself worked up. There'll be time later."

Their athair stood. "Let's take a leisurely flight, and I'll explain everything. I'm not sure your máthair wants your sisters to hear what I'm about to tell you. They're still too young to learn of such treachery."

Jaden's eyes narrowed. "Máthair knows too?"

After a terse nod, the older faeryman motioned toward the front door. "And now... *you* will." He closed the door behind them and headed for the local park. They flew in the dusky silence until they reached the black wrought iron gazebo in the rose garden. Except for the hum of their wings, all was silent. Even the normal sounds of nature had stilled.

A cold sensation niggled up Lylan's neck. The town had never been *this* quiet.

Chapter Nine

Once seated on a circle of toadstools inside the gazebo, their athair placed his elbows on his knees and folded his hands. Lylan surveyed his athair's face. The cold sensation he'd experienced on the way to the park eased. What was so intense that his grown sisters, though not quite yet of age, shouldn't hear? Lylan mirrored his athair's position and rested his chin in his left palm.

"Boys, your grandathair told this history to me and my friends around the time I'd become Lylan's age. Before I married your máthair and he became my athair-in-law. Our township, Glistineare, was once part of a great city called Glorianderis. Around eight thousand years ago, people drifted apart. The wealthy from the poor."

"How so?" Lylan cocked his head.

"Attitudes. According to your grandathair Estallan, who was around Jaden's age at the time, shy of two thousand years, King Noraldis was a worthy ruler. The king warned his people against forming prejudices.

"Before Prince Andreager reached maturity, the king had little time to spend with his son. Andreager didn't share his athair's attributes. The young prince was nearly of age when his máthair passed on. After her death, he became a cruel young faeryman, no doubt influenced by those with whom he hung around. He belittled his athair's love for their subjects and his efforts to improve their lives.

"Your grandathair watched as the king set off to visit a nearby town with needed materials after a major fire swept through the area. Prince Andreager stayed behind. His friends spread the word that the prince would be busy running the royal residence and not come out until his athair returned. Later, your grandathair had doubts about his seclusion. His two younger brothers and three sisters remained unseen as well.

"The king had left in a carriage, towing a wagon. He was gone longer than had been expected. Shadair Vanderrissian sent guards to search for their ruler. All hope that a broken wheel on the conveyance or other such mishap had caused the delay was dashed when the troop came upon the coach at the bottom of a ravine. The horses gone. The monarch's body was found along the shore and brought home."

Lylan had hung on every word. He pulled his jaw back into place and glimpsed his brother's open mouth. What a horrible tragedy. As his athair continued with the story, Lylan took in a deep breath.

"A few days later, Prince Andreager assumed the throne." Athair exhaled and tightened his lips. "The new King Andreager proclaimed his brothers and sisters were ambassadors placed in far outlying towns to serve the realm. No one ever heard from them again. After several weeks, the carriage horses were discovered back in the stables.

"As time went by, the city's upper class migrated closer to the castle, held their parties, and lived their lives above and separate from everyone else because of their prejudices. The rest of the residents moved to the other side of Emeraldis Pond. Our town of Glistineare was born.

"Those who formed the village of Amythaseah showed no respect to the people here. Food and everything else in our town were scarce. Speculation arose that Andreager had commandeered incoming supplies and left the residents of Glistineare on their own to live off the land. These conditions continued for another thousand years."

Lylan's athair leaned back on the gazebo's rail. "One night, King Andreager threw a huge gala event for his birthday. As the evening came into full swing, a tiny faeryling wandered into what had now become the royal palace. She wasn't much bigger than a firefly, only able to take small steps. She entered the ballroom and giggled. The music stopped. All eyes focused on her. The king exploded with fury that someone would bring the *creature* into his presence without an invitation. He despised faerylings. He never spent time with his own son, who he'd placed in the care of servants.

"No one knew who the faeryling was or where she'd come from. He demanded the guards take her out of his village and leave her at the edge of Glistineare. *'Let the peasants figure out what to do with the creature,'* he commanded."

"That's horrible, Athair." Lylan gritted his teeth.

Jaden's eyes grew misty, and he shook his lowered head.

"It was cruel, but not unexpected by anyone. Two guards grasped the barely out-of-infancy faeryling, holding her by the shoulders on either side, her feet dangling off the ground. She cried as they approached the double doors. The light in the room dispersed as if afraid to shine.

"The head of the shadair's order, Vanderrissian, stepped into the ballroom. His elegant turquoise wings turned the color of a storm cloud. His silver locks rose into spikes, and his voice thundered across the room. *'King Andreager, you have committed your last crime against this realm. You and your cohorts in this hamlet you call Amythaseah are sentenced to become nonexistent to the rest of the world of Crystandavair until one of your descendants proves worthy to be a royal leader by acts of kindness.'*

"The shadair and the faeryling disappeared. The room grew darker, as if a massive thunderstorm hung over the village. The king left his gala in a rage, and the guests fled.

"After that night, everyone stayed within the walls of the village. When the shadair placed the curse on Amythaseah, it became invisible to the rest of the kingdom. Except, the shadair still loved the people and made sure their needs would be met. So the hamlet appears once every hundred years for seven days. During that break, they may leave Amythaseah for necessities, and others may enter with provisions. Any who leave must return before the end of the week, or they are lost forever to their home with no memory of who they are or from whence they came.

"No one wanted to wind up in a world lacking the comforts they'd become accustomed to. Those inside Amythaseah cared not a whit that no one outside their realm could see them or remember them except during the seven-day break. The Amythaseans were content living in isolation with their peers."

"But, Athair." Jaden flew off the toadstool. "How do you have knowledge of these events? How did Grandathair tell you? I thought he was in the city when it was cursed. Was he in the ballroom when it happened? How did he wind up in Glistineare? You said Máthair had been told of this?"

Lylan snatched Jaden's ankle and pulled him back onto the seat before his fluttering wings took him to the roof. "I'm sure Athair's not finished. Calm down." Lylan snickered. Had he been that flighty when younger?

His athair pursed his lips. "Yes, your máthair was told the story long ago." He took a deep breath. "Your grandathair is also a shadair. They can communicate with one another on a level few can understand. The Head Shadair, Vanderrissian, who chose to live in the realm of Amythaseah, sent your grandathair Estallan to

Glistineare. Vanderrissian later got word to Estallan of everything that had transpired after he left the village.

"After the first one thousand years of the curse, Vanderrissian perceived more changes in the people of Amythaseah. Some, especially the king, wanted more than his needs met. Talk became hostile. The shadair feared what might happen during the next break in the hundred-year disappearance. He gave warning to others outside the hamlet of the anticipated danger for those seven days.

"King Andreager directed hunting parties to gather slaves for his kingdom.

"After the next hundred-year break, when the guards returned from their raid, Shadair Vanderrissian placed a curse on Andreager for his cruelty and selfishness. The king died in his sleep that night, and his son, Farmeran, was crowned.

"This ruler had a kind heart because of the way the servant raised him. King Farmeran planned to change things in the realm in hopes he'd reverse the curse.

"But Prince Maricent, the king's son, followed in his grandathair, King Andreager's footsteps.

"When King Farmeran's wife died, Princess Shamera was given a caring nurse to raise her. The very young princess thrived. Prince Maricent, being much older, was put in the care of a servant who became disgruntled with the monarch. The servant put evil thoughts into the prince's head. Those, along with the notions formed from reading about the deeds of his grandathair, King Andreager, caused him to hate his athair.

"The other day, Estallan warned me that Prince Maricent will be crowned king in Amythaseah within the next few days because of his athair's disappearance during the village's last seven-day period of visibility one hundred years ago. Shadair Vanderrissian had opposed the prince's ascension to the throne in the hopes King Farmeran would be found. Yet now... he's given in to the request."

Lylan shook his head, his eyes shut. "I'm sorry to interrupt, Athair, but do I have this straight? Grandathair has been gone for a hundred years, as has the King of Amythaseah, according to what you said. And both incidents happened the last time this village appeared across Emeraldis Pond. That can't be a coincidence." He blinked at his athair. "And, this history was seen firsthand or told later to Grandathair, who was actually a shadair. How have you received this information after our grandathair disappeared? Are you a shadair too?"

"Seems so, although I have no idea how much of the powers work. And Estallan hasn't indicated where he is, though I do have my suspicions. He is instructing me. Messages come to me most often in dreams. To assure me it's him contacting me, he includes a piece of information about our family no one else would know. That's why I warned you and Jaden to be home before twilight." He narrowed his eyes at Lylan. "Which instruction, I remind you, you *did not* obey."

Lylan gave him a sheepish grin. Thought he'd escaped this lecture. "Yes, Athair. I apologize. We should have started for home earlier, but then what might have happened to the faerylet who stumbled into our camp?"

"Ah, yes. Perhaps these events were meant to be, my boy."

"Athair?" Jaden pulled a lop-sided smile. "Whatever happened to the little faeryling who crashed the king's event?" He shrugged, and his wings fluttered, raising him off the seat.

"Son. Settle down, or you'll tangle your hair in the rafters. You're too excitable."

"He sure is." Lylan chuckled. One of these days, those emotions would cause his brother a heap of trouble.

"Why does everyone always tell me that?" Jaden drifted back to the seat. "So, what happened to her?"

"I don't know. Right now, we can't dwell on the faeryling. We have to prepare." Their athair rose from the toadstool.

Lylan stood. "Prepare for what?"

Rustling and gruff voices in the bushes surrounding the town's central garden distracted the three faerymen. The hairs on Lylan's neck prickled.

Chapter Ten

Six faery guards in golden garb burst through the bushes and rushed toward Lylan, his brother, and athair. Who were they? Where did they come from? Lylan squinted at the emblem on their tunics. The insignia was the same crest he'd observed on the gates of the purple village.

Lylan dodged one guard, who lunged to grab him. *Why have they attacked us? We've done nothing to them.*

His athair twirled into the air toward two faery attackers who had secured Jaden's hands and wings. Athair's feet slammed into the jaws of the guards, rendering them senseless for the moment.

Lylan bolted forward into another gold-clad faery's stomach. The guard doubled over and groaned. Jaden yanked a sapling from the dirt. With roots trailing behind, he used the pliable small tree as a whip, smashing it over the head of a fourth assailant until he wobbled. The remaining two fled through the woods, followed by each of the beaten guards.

"What in blinking bluebells was that all about?" Jaden stood beside their athair, the tree held upright like a staff.

"This was a raiding party, wasn't it?" Lylan turned to his athair. "One of those you told us of... from Amythaseah."

"It may have been more than just a raiding party, son. Let's go back to the house and talk to the lass you brought home."

Chapter Eleven

*A*s the three faerymen approached their home, Lylan's pulse sped up. The house shouldn't be dark. No sound anywhere, not even from the forest. Though it was nightfall, Máthair wouldn't have retired. Not until they returned. Another chill ran up his spine, into his neck, and across his shoulders to his wings, which vibrated like a plucked harp string. The hair on his nape bristled. "Athair." He grabbed his athair's and brother's arms, then whispered, "Something's not right."

"No, it's not." He drew Lylan and Jaden into the thicket. "Stay here while I investigate." He glanced at Lylan. "I believe you're developing some of those senses your grandathair and I have. Keep calm and listen. See if you can detect any sounds or voices while I move closer to the house."

"Okay, but I don't like you going alone."

"I don't like it either." Jaden's wings flapped in a frenzied blur. "Why don't I go with you?"

His athair smiled. "Thank you, son, but with your excitability, you'd give me away. Remain here with Lylan and try to stay calm."

Jaden peered at his brother. He pursed his lips. "I can't wait to come of age. Will this nervous habit end by then?"

As their athair disappeared into the woods to approach the house from a more secluded area, Lylan patted Jaden's back. "I'm sure you'll outgrow it, little brother. Now let me concentrate and see if I can hear anything, as Athair requested."

Lylan closed his eyes. Different levels of breathing. Some from the house and others from the woods his athair had entered. A gruff, gravelly voice whispered. What was he saying? *"Let him pass, and we'll follow him to the house."*

"Jaden. Hurry. Athair's fallen into a trap."

Chapter Twelve

*L*ylan and Jaden headed in the direction their athair had gone. No one was on the trail. Lylan slowed his wings and lighted on the ground, his senses alert. His brother followed, but his wings still fluttered anxiously.

"Jaden, calm yourself before we're caught. Either Athair went into the house, or he took a different path." *Unlikely.*

The sound of a scuffle reached Lylan's ears. "Behind the house. Let's go."

The two brothers took off in a flash, leaving a trail of faery dust behind them. They rounded the end of the thicket near the back door of their home and descended into the bushes. Four faerymen, dressed in the same garb as those the brothers had tangled with earlier, had tied their athair's wings, arms, legs, and ankles. They each held on to him and flew to the rear door of the cottage. One guard kicked in the door.

As they dragged Lylan's athair into the house, raised voices, with indistinguishable words, filled the air. Jaden started for the door.

"*No.* Wait. Máthair and our sisters must be gagged. That means they must be bound as well."

"Quiet, you three!" a gruff voice yelled.

Jaden grabbed his brother's biceps. "What shall we do? We can't sit here and do nothing. If what Athair told us is right, those guards will take our family to the vanishing village, and they'll become slaves. We have to stop them."

"Yes. We must, and we will. I have a plan."

Lylan explained what he had in mind, and Jaden nodded. Through the cover of bushes, they approached the back of the cottage, slipped around the corner, and crouched in a row of shrubs under a side window to the main room. Lylan peered in.

Inside the house, their athair, máthair, and two sisters had been tied to kitchen chairs and placed against the far wall. His athair sat under the window opposite where the brothers hid. His máthair had a deep red bruise on her cheek. They'd struck her. The hair on both his female siblings was tangled as if they'd been roughed up too. Heat rose in Lylan's neck as he gritted his teeth. Blood oozed from his athair's forehead.

One of the guards asked, "What do you suppose happened to those two younger faerymen?"

The guard who appeared to be in charge of the group glared at him. "I *told* you four to keep sentry outside the front and back doors. Get out there. Those two must be around somewhere. Take Stancian with you. Five should be enough to handle those two Glistineareans. Two in the front and three in the back. *Now! Out!*"

Lylan glanced at his brother. "These shrubs are tall enough to conceal us while we wait for our chance." He peered over the windowsill, hidden by the untrimmed bushes. He held his index finger to his lips to hush his brother and his whooshing wings. Jaden pulled them forward and latched onto the tips. Lylan smiled and nodded. Jaden grinned. *Little brother is learning.*

Without a sound, Lylan inched to the corner of the house nearest the front door. He waited.

Two guards slipped out and took positions on either side. Lylan slowed his breathing. After a visual canvas of the area, the guards leaned against the wall and chatted.

Lylan moved back to the window and found Jaden returning from the other corner of the house. Jaden whispered, "I checked the back door. Three faerymen guards. Looks like they've settled in for a boring task of sentry duty. Hadn't even looked around."

His brother was smart and coming of age fast. Didn't have to instruct him to do anything. Lylan patted Jaden's back. His brother's wings stayed calm as a spring night. "Good job. This is the break we need. Wait here while I fly over the roof to the window across the room where they have Athair bound. I'll slip my pocket knife into Athair's hands through the opening. When I return, we'll wait until he frees his hands. Then we'll rush in through this window and subdue the guard."

"Right." Jaden gave him a thumbs-up.

Lylan peeked in through the window again.

The inside guard's gruff voice grated on Lylan's nerves. "You four will either cooperate, or I won't be responsible for what happens to these pretty little faerylets. Where is Lady Jillian? We *may* decide to spare you from a life of slavery in Amythaseah if you comply."

Lady Jillian? He must mean the faerylet they brought home. Taking a deep breath to calm his spirit, he leaned in close to Jaden's ear. "Stay here and keep an eye on the inside guard. Do what you have to if he touches our sisters or máthair. I'll be right back."

In silence, Lylan zoomed over the roof and came down on the other side. He dared not peek through the window with the guard standing right in front of his athair.

Spitu

Had Máthair spit at the guard? He'd better not touch her.

Crack

He hit her. Lylan crouched, about to burst through the window straight for the guard's throat.

Creeeaak

He stilled. That sounded like the squeak made by the secret wall panel Athair had created for them to hide in when danger was near.

"Leave her alone, Krostun. Here I am."

Lylan risked a glance through the window. The guard had turned to face Lady Jillian as she stepped into the room.

"Take me back to Amythaseah if you must. I'll marry your precious prince and give up my freedom. I'd rather endure my fate with him than have Tally subjected to his cruelty since you captured her before she could even leave the village. Leave these kind souls alone." Jillian swung her hand around, indicating the Chaldres.

Krostun seized her and whipped a rope from his belt around her wings and arms. "Nobody gives me orders. I'll do as I wish." He laughed. "Precious prince. Right. Maybe I'll tell him we found you dead and keep you hidden for myself. He'll have to accept your washed-out friend if he wants to be crowned. I can mollify him with a gift of these peasants. He won't believe anything these rustics say."

Lylan zipped through the open window, slipped his knife into his athair's bound hands, and charged Krostun while the guard's back remained turned.

Chapter Thirteen

*L*ylan landed on Krostun's back. The guard twisted, and they fell to the floor, Lylan on top. Krostun struggled and kicked, grappling with Lylan to grab his wings, but the guard wasn't quick enough to manage a solid grip. Lylan wrestled Krostun onto his stomach and sat on him, the guard's arms and wings immobilized by Lylan's knees.

Jillian grabbed a length of twine and a knife from the hiding place and handed them to Lylan. She held the blade in front of Krostun's face for a moment. "I suggest you not move. I don't appreciate the way you threatened me or this wonderful family." The guard didn't flicker an eyelash, but fear spread across his face.

Dirty coward. Lylan chuckled. But then... she *was* quite the formidable faerylet.

Jillian glanced at him. "What?"

"Nothing. I wouldn't move either." He grinned.

The back door guards burst in. Jaden flew through the other door. Lylan's athair sliced through the last rope on his feet and grabbed the first guard, while the one they'd called Stancian secured the arms of the second.

As everyone's jaw lowered, their brows rose, and they stared at the guard named Stancian.

A smile spread across Stancian's face. He straightened his posture. "Before King Farmeran disappeared, he asked me to find out which guards were loyal to him. His Majesty had sensed unrest. I'd discovered some of the royal detachment had pledged fealty to Prince Maricent. I had planned to report my findings to Shadair Vanderrissian but was ordered on this detail before I could find him. This treason against our realm and the crimes against the world of Crystandavair had to be stopped, so I decided to tag along."

Lylan's instincts assured him he could trust Stancian. He glanced at his athair, who nodded.

After Lylan, Jaden, and their athair secured the captive guards, Stancian gazed around the room. His eyes lighted on the brothers' older sister, Daleah.

The guards from the front door sauntered into the room, eyes widened. Lylan snatched the dagger from Jillian. His athair flipped his blade from hand to hand. Stancian pulled his sword out and tossed a second to Jaden. The two guards dropped their weapons without a fight.

Stancian released Lylan's máthair and the girls from their bonds. He beamed at Daleah. She returned his smile.

"Our town magistrate will know what to do," Lylan suggested. "Since it's not yet morning, we'll take these miscreants to the gaol and have the night gaoler, Bostair, hold them until the magistrate is available."

Stancian's brows furrowed. "Will they be secure? No way to escape?"

Lylan nodded. "You can count on it. Bostair hasn't lost a prisoner on the graveyard shift in all the years he's held the position. My athair and Jaden can stay here and protect Máthair, our sisters, and Lady Jillian." He glanced at the beautiful faerylet and back to Stancian. "Just in case any more scum try something. You and I should be enough to handle this bunch of traitors and deliver them to the gaol."

Sharon K Connell

Chapter Fourteen

After the guards were placed in cells, Lylan told Bostair everything that had happened. "I sense I should stay."

Stancian thumped Lylan on his shoulder. "If you stay, so shall I. To make sure those miscreants don't pull something during the night."

"I appreciate your both staying." Bostair nodded to Lylan and Stancian. "We've not had more than three offenders in here at a time since we built the gaol. And that time, it was only for three brothers held in contempt by the judge during a clan dispute. Where did these faerymen come from?"

"It's a long story." Lylan grinned at Stancian, whose lips rose on one side in a cockeyed smile.

"Well, it's not like we have much else to do here outside of playing checkers." Bostair leaned the chair back and lifted his feet to the desk.

Lylan chuckled. "You're right." He settled in the wooden seat across from the gaoler. Stancian pulled another chair from against the wall and joined the two. Lylan told Bostair the entire story they'd heard from their athair that night.

"Wow." Bostair's light brown eyes grew as round as hazelnuts. "You're saying these treasonous guards came from Amythaseah? When the elders had no idea I was listening, they mentioned a strange place that appears across the pond, but I've never seen the purple village."

The door to the gaol inched open. Lylan, Stancian, and Bostair jumped to their feet, weapons drawn.

Jillian stepped into the room. Her eyes grew to saucer size, and she gasped.

Lylan sheathed his sword and extended his hand. "It's okay. We didn't expect you. With the excitement around here, we were never formally introduced. I'm Lylan Chaldre. You were staying in my parents' home after you fainted in the woods."

Stancian and Bostair retook their places.

She pushed the covered platter, with the aroma of succulent roasted vegetables, which permeated the air, toward Lylan. "Your máthair wanted to make sure you both had something to eat after tonight's activity. Since she attended to my feet and bound them, I'm almost as good as new. I told her I'd fly here and deliver your food so she could take care of your family. She gave me directions where to find you."

He accepted the plate with a smile. Her cheeks flushed, and she lowered her gaze. "My name is... Jillian."

Lylan placed the platter on the officer's desk. "From what I overheard the guard we subdued say, you're *Lady* Jillian... from Amythaseah." He turned to her and swung his hand toward the seat he'd occupied before she made her appearance.

Jillian lowered herself to the chair, adjusting her glittering white wings. "I was. But not anymore. I've left my life in the palace to find a more normal one."

Stancian's brows knit. His expression saddened.

Lylan pulled another chair up next to her. "Have you eaten anything since I brought you home?"

She shook her head. "My stomach is tied in knots. I don't think I can."

"You have to try. It might settle your nerves. Máthair is a genius at preparing food you'd *die* for." He winced at his choice of words. "I mean, no one cooks better than she does."

"All right." She placed the tote bag from her side on the floor and set out two dishes and tableware. She also brought out a flask and a couple of tulip-shaped glasses. "You and Stancian go ahead and eat first. You've had a rough night."

"We can share." Lylan placed a serving of the roasted and seasoned vegetables, dripping with sauce, on each side of his plate. "Bostair, if you have another dish around here, there's enough for everyone."

"Sure do. I'll not pass up an offer to partake of your máthair's cooking. Mmm mmm." He popped out of his seat and headed for a back room.

The front door opened again. Lylan and Stancian spun, ready for battle, hands on their weapons. The old gentlefaeryman, Fyan, who had shown up at the Chaldres' doorstep a hundred years ago, froze.

"Sorry to startle you, sirs. I have the gaoler's breakfast. The cook said to bring the food. He's prompt with serving meals. Bostair will be off duty soon. I didn't realize he'd have company." After he'd spoken the clipped sentences, his hands shook and rattled the platter's metal cover.

Jillian sprang from her place, her mouth agape. "*Your Majesty.*" She fell into a deep curtsy while Stancian sank one knee to the floor and bowed his head.

Chapter Fifteen

*L*ylan stared at Fyan dressed in hand-me-downs from various families. The day he and his brother found the aged faeryman on the doorstep of their home in the wee hours of the morning, his clothing had been ripped to shreds. Worse than Jillian's when she stumbled out of the bushes last night. Fyan told them he'd wandered through the forest. The poor soul had no idea where he was nor who he was.

Fyan murmured, "Stand up, faerylet. I'm not royalty."

As his gaze strayed to Jillian, Lylan lost himself in her dazzling flaxen hair.

She remained in an unwavering curtsy before Fyan. "You are King Farmeran, Sire."

Fyan shuffled to the desk. He lowered the plate, turned, and took Jillian's arm in hand, pulling her to her feet. "Faerylet. Do I look like royalty to you?"

Lylan's brows knit. This old gentlefaeryman couldn't be a king. Although... when he and Jaden found him, he had been garbed in deep purple. His green and golden wings were bent and dirty as if he'd been in a fight. Could it be? *Is he really a king?* Athair said anyone who didn't return to the village of Amythaseah would lose their memory. But why had Fyan been in such terrible physical condition?

Tears filled Jillian's eyes. "You don't remember, Your Majesty. You left the village. When you didn't return before the curse took effect again, you lost your memory. You *are* King Farmeran. You and my athair were best friends. He was your royal councilman. Please try to remember. What happened to you?"

Lylan's athair entered the gaol. "I worried about this young faerylet when she didn't come back to the house." His focus bounced from Jillian to Fyan to Lylan. "Is everything okay here? Are the guards locked up? Where's Bostair?"

The gaoler opened the backroom door. His eyes grew round. "Well, this sure has turned into a party."

"Athair, I invited... ah... Lady Jillian, Stancian, and Bostair to share my meal, but Fyan... or His Majesty... or—anyway, he brought Bostair's food... and *Lady* Jillian and Stancian said Fyan is King Farmeran from Amythaseah." Lylan caught his breath. He hadn't spewed such a mouthful of gibberish since he was a faeryling. What must Jillian think of him? "Can this be, Athair? Is Fyan the king of Amythaseah?"

As Lylan's athair tapped his finger on his chin, he circled Fyan. "That explains what your grandathair told me in a dream months ago. He spoke of a crown and a lost king. But I failed to comprehend." Lylan's athair turned to his son. "I guess you've discovered the identity of our house guest as well."

With a crash, Fyan fell to the floor. His skin paled. Jillian rushed to him and felt his forehead. "He must be sick. He's clammy. If someone can tell me where I can stay, I'll take care of him, but we have to find help."

Lylan joined her next to Fyan. "Lady Jillian, Athair will bring my máthair to care for him."

His athair flew out of the doorway without a word. Bostair rushed to the back room. Stancian ladled a dipper of water from the wooden barrel in the corner of the room. He grabbed a napkin from the table and dabbed Fyan's forehead with the moistened cloth.

"Please, Lylan." Jillian pleaded. "Stop calling me *Lady*."

While Bostair returned with a blanket and pillow, Lylan asked Jillian, "Are you sure this is the king of Amythaseah?"

She placed the pillow under the monarch's head and covered him with Lylan's help, then stood and turned weepy eyes on Lylan. "I am certain. As I said, I was Lady Jillian. My athair and King Farmeran, his best friend, vanished when they left the village together one hundred years ago."

As if a dam had burst, Jillian's story gushed from her lips.

"My máthair said Prince Maricent demanded my hand in marriage, so he could be crowned King of Amythaseah according to law. If I had stayed, I'd have had to marry the prince this week. King Farmeran is a wonderful ruler. His son is terrible. I'd be nothing more than a servant to him, so I ran away. My heart broke as I left my máthair, but she would've stopped me. Máthair said to be chosen by the prince was an honor. She tried to convince me that, as queen, I'd hold a position of authority. She was deceived. I don't care if I forget everything. I'd rather become the king's servant here in your town. Please don't send me back." The color drained from her face, and she dropped to her knees before the monarch.

"Why can't you both go back to the village? His memory might come back. Surely he wouldn't make you go through with the wedding. He's still the king."

"His word would mean nothing. He can't remember who he is. The high council will declare him unfit to rule. Walking back through the gates will not alter the curse." Tears flowed over Jillian's cheeks. "Please, let me stay and take care of the king."

The gaol's front door opened again.

Lylan's eyes narrowed. Now, who was this? Someone else he'd have to fight from the purple village? His brows lowered. This was no guard. Not with those robes. The old faeryman reminded Lylan of his grandathair but more distinctive with his turquoise wings and silver hair. "Who are you?"

"Shadair Vanderrissian?" Jillian swiped the tears from her eyes and rose.

"My dear. Everything is fine." The shadair's face glowed.

Chapter Sixteen

hat had this odd faeryman with the long beard meant? That Jillian was okay? Lylan searched the ancient wrinkled face with a sharp nose but kind eyes. Was he really a shadair?

With a wave of the shadair's hand, King Farmeran's color returned. He sat up and shook his head. "What happened? Where am I?" He gazed at Jillian with clouded eyes. "Lady Jillian? Why are you here? Are you all right?"

"Oh, King Farmeran. You remember?" She again felt his forehead. "His fever is gone." She whipped her head around to the shadair. "Will His Majesty be back to normal now?"

The shadair's entire face lit up with a grin, and his eyes twinkled. "He'll be fine, my lady. So will everyone else in Amythaseah... as soon as we return."

Lylan's eyes narrowed. What was he talking about?

Once more, the door opened, and in flew Lylan's parents. His athair glanced at King Farmeran with a puzzled look. "You're well?"

"I believe so." The king's expression matched those on both of Lylan's athair and máthair.

She stepped forward and felt the king's forehead. "It would seem my services are not needed here. I have work to do at home."

"Please stay." The shadair moved a long bench up to the desk. "You should hear what I'm about to say too."

The couple lowered themselves to the seat.

"I don't understand what's happened." Lylan pinned the shadair with a stare. "Would you please explain?"

"Of course, Lylan."

"What?" Lylan's brows rumpled. "You know my name?"

"We shadairs know many things. I've watched you for a long time, my boy. Your grandathair speaks highly of you. Before I explain everything, eat. Perhaps you can set a plate for the king too. He looks like he could use it."

No one moved. They stared at the ancient faery.

"I insist." With the expression of a schoolmaster, the shadair glanced at each one in the room with piercing eyes.

Everyone took a seat at the desk. The savory roasted vegetables were passed and divided among them. Except to the shadair, who declined to eat while he spoke.

While the others munched on their meal and kept their eyes glued to the shadair, he adjusted his robes and began. "You're aware of the curse I laid on the village of Amythaseah. I'd had enough of King Andreager's cruelty. I wanted to whisk away the faeryling, who happened to be my great-granddaughter. But the evil in our village had to be controlled before it spread to the entire world of Crystandavair. So, I allowed the scene to play out and then cast the spell."

He strode across the room. "Later, when my anger had subsided, I realized the hamlet needed not only supplies but influence from the outside. The curse remained, except for seven days once every one hundred years." The shadair circled the desk.

"I also made a shadair's decree, one not to be broken, not by the monarch or *even* me. I said the village would remain under the curse until one of the king's descendants proved himself or... *herself* worthy to be a royal leader by acts of kindness."

Vanderrissian kneeled at Jillian's side. "You, my dear princess, have done that."

Lylan's mouth dropped open. She was... a *princess*... not just a lady? He'd carried a *princess* in his arms. His pulse sped to high gear, his eyes riveted to Jillian.

Her jaw lowered. She shook her head. "I'm not one of King Andreager's descendants. My athair was a duke, Lord Raynar."

Shadair Vanderrissian stood and smiled down at her. "I know exactly who your athair is. He doesn't. Yet."

"Is? Doesn't? I assumed my athair was dead, or he'd have come home to be with us. He'd never let me be sold to Prince Maricent."

"No. If... he'd been able to stop the event. Your athair is alive, dear. He's been held captive in the dungeon ever since the prince tricked his athair into a charitable mission outside Amythaseah one hundred years ago."

She flicked her eyes at Lylan and back to the shadair. "And you didn't help him?" Her eyes and stance reflected the horror on her face. "Why not?"

"At first, I wasn't aware of your athair's capture. When I found out King Farmeran was still alive, I searched for your athair without success. The king had already lost his memory by then. To bring him back would have changed nothing... as I believe you mentioned a while ago.

"Years later, I learned from a servant that two faerymen were held in the dungeon. I discovered Shadair Estallan had been locked up after a raid on this village." Vanderrissian turned to Lylan. "Your grandathair informed me the other faeryman was Lord Raynar."

Tears swelled in Jillian's eyes. Lylan longed to hold her close and comfort her. But the shadair said she was a princess. A romantic relationship with her was beyond his reach.

As the shadair cleared his throat, Lylan brought his attention back to the ancient faeryman.

Vanderrissian winked at Lylan. "It was time to bring things back to a place where everyone would live their lives in peace and joy. So I waited. I did not foresee Maricent's treachery with his raids and plan to take Jillian against her will. But his plans are of no consequence now."

Shadair Vanderrissian lowered himself next to Jillian once more. "Your athair maintained his loyalty to King Farmeran. And you have much to learn about your athair."

The king nodded and murmured, "Yes. *Lord* Raynar was loyal."

Lylan peered at the ruler, whose eyes looked as though a cloud had lifted from them.

Vanderrissian rose and placed a hand on the king's shoulder. "That's right, Your Majesty. *Lord Raynar.* Your closest advisor and friend."

Again, the king nodded. A smile spread across his face.

The shadair patted King Farmeran's shoulder. "What no one in the kingdom has been aware of is this. Raynar was the babe the queen gave birth to when she died. *Lord* Raynar is King Andreager's brother."

The king's eyes widened.

Shadair Vanderrissian removed his hand from the monarch's shoulder and paced as he continued. "Because of the queen's death, King Noraldis hadn't announced his new son's birth to the kingdom before he was murdered. Two others knew of the birth but, by law, couldn't say anything. The sovereign had to order the announcement."

Vanderrissian stopped in front of Lylan. "The doctor who delivered the infant and the babe's nurse alone were privy to the birth. Or so it was thought. But Prince Andreager had eavesdropped at his máthair's chamber when she died in the delivery of his new brother. He had no tears for his máthair. Even less concern for another prince in the kingdom who might usurp him.

"A fire broke out in the province. King Noraldis was determined to deliver aid to those affected. He needed to stay busy after the loss of his queen, so he went himself. It was the perfect time for Andreager to set his plan in motion."

The shadair's wings darkened. His eyes held sparks as if a lightning storm brewed in them. "Prince Andreager ordered assassins to kill the king. They succeeded. He also had his máthair's doctor and the babe's nurse meet with *accidents* to keep his secret.

Then he turned to Prince Raynar." Vanderrissian paused. "But even Andreager couldn't kill an infant faeryling.

"He put a nobleman's family in charge of Prince Raynar and told them he was the queen's beloved nurse's faerylet. Andreager told the couple they were never to reveal the *truth* about the babe and to raise him as their own. Under penalty of death. The lord had daughters but no sons. He made Raynar his heir. The old couple you called your grandparents before they passed were actually your athair's adoptive parents."

The shadair continued his pacing, his wings even darker. "Prince Andreager didn't know the nurse present at Raynar's birth was my granddaughter. He had ordered a guard to shove her out of the tower window. I'd been meditating in the woods beyond the palace when my granddaughter's screams came to my ears. I found her right before she died. She told me of Raynar's birth and who caused her death. She had overheard the prince's plans to have a noble family secretly take Raynar as their son." Vanderrissian spun and faced the others.

"I was furious. My granddaughter was dead. Her wee faeryling máthairless. Prince Raynar had been sold. As I stormed toward the palace doors, a strong, positive sensation came to me. Let Andreager think he's won. Time will pass. And one day, everything will come together to make things right. Of course, Andreager died not much longer after that."

He gazed into Jillian's eyes. "Now the time has come. Your athair grew up as a lord and never dreamed he was heir to the throne. Something told me things were better left that way. Treachery would lie ahead for Raynar as he grew older if it were known he was a prince of the realm."

Lylan marveled as the shadair's wings returned to their brilliant shades of turquoise. What a complicated mess. Jillian's... *Princess* Jillian's athair should be the monarch, not King Farmeran.

Vanderrissian stopped in front of her. "You *are* of royal blood. The kind deeds shown to King Farmeran and this worthy family— *my* family—have broken the curse."

"Whoa!" The word came out of Lylan's mouth before he realized he'd said anything. *His family?* What did he mean by that?

Chapter Seventeen

ylan pressed his lips together. The curse wasn't the only thing broken this day. He hung his head and drew in a deep breath. He'd known Jillian for a single day, but he'd fallen in love with her already. Would his heart ever heal? She'd go back to Amythaseah while he lived out his life alone.

A thought jolted him. "Shadair Vanderrissian?"

"Yes?"

"You said my grandathair is in a dungeon?"

"That's right. You can all put your minds at rest. When Maricent's guards left King Farmeran for dead and captured *Lord* Raynar, Shadair Estallan witnessed the treachery. Estallan attempted to sneak away unseen to find help, but a guard spotted him. He and Raynar have kept each other uplifted all these years. Your grandathair kept sending messages to your athair, hoping something could be done to release them and turn things around for the village. We'll return to the hamlet tomorrow and clean up Prince Maricent's mess. Then everything will be set to right."

Lylan's máthair had tears in her eyes.

His athair rose from his seat. "No wonder I received messages from my athair-in-law. How is it I've developed powers as a shadair? There are none in my family."

Shadair Vanderrissian laughed. "Estallan never had a son. You've become close, and since there are no female shadairs," Vanderrissian glanced at Fedreta, "Estallan made you his apprentice until Lylan is experienced enough."

Lylan's heart filled with joy for his athair despite the ache at the thought of losing Jillian.

"We'll need rest for the trip back to Amythaseah." Vanderrissian glanced around the room, and his eyes rested on Bostair. "Be assured, your detainees won't go anywhere until tomorrow. I've secured the cells with a spell, so no one can open them. We'll take the captives with us when we leave."

Bostair sighed. "I humbly thank you, Shadair Vanderrissian. I'd not want a black mark on my record, and I'm sure my relief this morning will be happy regardless of how long the prisoners remain here." He waved to everyone as they left the gaolhouse and closed the door.

As Lylan fell in beside Jillian on their return to the house, his heart grew heavier with each step.

Sharon K Connell

Chapter Eighteen

Sunlight streamed into the room as Jillian opened her eyes the next morning. She arose, made her bed, washed, and dressed. Her room companions, Daleah and Merrilee, were gone. Princess or not, she should have gotten up earlier to assist with breakfast preparation.

After a delicious morning meal, Jillian helped with cleanup and returned to the bedroom. She couldn't bear the sad way Lylan gazed at her. Had he guessed how attracted she was to him? How she hated the idea of leaving this wonderful town... and him.

As her memory strayed, she recalled how he'd come to his family's rescue and saved her from the cruel guard, Krostun.

Butterflies filled her stomach, and flew in a frenzy. How could she have such deep feelings for a faeryman she'd met mere days ago? Yet, she couldn't deny them. How would she survive without him?

A knock sounded on the door. Daleah stuck her head in before she and Merrilee entered the room.

Daleah swung a gown from her arms. "We've brought you a change of attire for the journey home." She pointed to the dress in her sister's arms. "Your choice. You're the same size as both of us, so we each chose a gown for you. We're sure you have far better in Amythaseah, but at least these are fresh. Please take your pick."

Jillian smiled at the two sisters, who she'd also grown close to in the last two days. They were so dear, even before they found out she was a princess.

The faerylets laid out their pink and green dresses on the bed Jillian had slept in. Pink had always been her favorite color, but since Daleah had given her one yesterday... "I'll wear this mint-colored one of Merrilee's today. Thank you so much for your kindness." Her eyes moistened. "I'll never forget it... or either of you."

Both sisters beamed as Daleah said, "We enjoyed having you here with us for these couple of days."

Merrilee nodded and ducked her head. Her cheeks glowed with the same shade of rose in her wings.

"I can never repay the kindness you, your parents, and your brothers have shown me. Visit me in Amythaseah. We've some very fine shoppes you and your máthair would appreciate."

After she changed, Jillian stepped into the living space of the Chaldres' home. Her eyes locked on Lylan's and misted when he smiled. *How can this be?* Her heart broke at the thought of leaving here—leaving him. *He's everything I've always dreamed of in a faeryman. Yet, he's letting me go.*

A rap came at the door, and Jaden rushed to answer.

Shadair Vanderrissian swept into the room, followed by Stancian. Jillian's heart ached. Time to leave. "I guess I'm ready to go home now." She fought back a torrent of tears.

As he touched her shoulder, the shadair smiled at her. "We will not travel alone."

He addressed Lylan's athair. "The guards who accompanied me to your town will have their hands full with our captives on the journey. Would you allow your sons to accompany us to Amythaseah? They've proven to be fine protectors. I'd be much more at ease with added security."

Lylan's athair glanced at them, then Jillian. He grinned at the shadair. "If they're willing, they have my blessing. They *have* shown themselves capable in time of need." He patted Lylan and Jaden on their backs.

The brothers raised their brows.

Lylan turned to Jillian, a warm smile on his lips.

Heat flooded her neck and cheeks. He wanted to go with them. But perhaps she'd read too much into his smile.

Chapter Nineteen

*L*ylan's heart pounded like the base drum in the town band at the midsummer celebration. She'd returned his smile. Did that mean she was happy he'd join her on the journey home? Didn't matter. Who was he to think he had a right to win the hand of a princess? "Come, Jaden. Let's throw together the things we'll need for the journey."

Jaden followed his brother to the loft, where they shared a room.

Lylan tossed a sack for their clothes to Jaden. "Only a two-day trip if all goes well." Jillian's tattered clothes, when she'd stumbled into their camp, came to Lylan's mind. She was so beautiful. How gorgeous she'd be in her royal raiment.

He tossed a tunic onto his cot. Once they returned home, he'd never see Jillian again. His chest tightened as if an anvil sat upon it.

The brothers returned to the main room. Their máthair rushed to them and hugged each. "You *will* be careful?"

Jaden dropped his sack of belongings to the floor and embraced his máthair. He turned to the shadair. "Sir, I've one more question about what happened so long ago."

"And what is that, my boy?" The shadair placed his hand on Jaden's shoulder.

"You never told us what became of the little faeryling, your great-granddaughter, after you cursed the village at King Andreager's celebration. Is she okay? Those guards were pretty rough with such a little one. Is she alive and well... and happy?"

The shadair focused on Fedreta. "I believe she has been *extremely* happy. I didn't want King Andreager to take his revenge on my family, so I removed them from the village. They lived their lives in beautiful towns with caring fairies around them but with no memory of unhappy days in Amythaseah. Everything should come back now that the curse is lifted."

He held out his hand to their máthair. "Do you remember, Fedreta?"

Lylan and Jaden stared open-mouthed at their máthair.

With eyelashes touching her brows, her eyes widened, and her jaw dropped. "Great-grandathair?" She flew into the shadair's arms.

Lylan's breath hitched. "Our máthair is *your* great-granddaughter?" His gaze traveled from the shadair to his máthair, to his athair, and to each faery in the room.

"Well, this sure is a surprise." Stancian's brows almost reached his black hairline.

Lylan freed the lungful of air he'd gulped in. "I'll say." He eyed the shadair. "That means I'm your—"

"Correct, my boy." Shadair Vanderrissian waved his arm around toward Jaden, Daleah, Merrilee, and their parents. "You are *all* my family."

A peace settled over Lylan. *So that was what he'd meant by his family when we were about to leave the gaol.*

The shadair slapped Lylan on the back. "Now, let us depart. We must arrive in Amythaseah before nightfall. I have much to do to set everything in order, starting with the release of your athair, Princess Jillian." He nodded to her, then turned to Lylan. "And your grandathair, my grandson-in-law. Yes, Estallan was the husband of my granddaughter, who died at the hand of Prince Andreager, and your máthair was the child she left máthairless, the faeryling who wandered into Andreager's party."

While Lylan and the others stared at Vanderrissian with eyes as big as a hoot owl's, the shadair strode to the door. "Let's hope we don't run across any more of Prince Maricent's guards on our way to Amythaseah."

Chapter Twenty

As the king's entourage set off through the forest bound for Emeraldis Pond, Shadair Vanderrissian led the way, followed by his guards, who flanked the detainees. Behind them, King Farmeran kept pace with Princess Jillian.

At the back of the group, Lylan studied the shadows in the woods. "Jaden, you and I should take the rear while Stancian and the rest of the guards monitor the captives."

Jaden grasped his arm. "You need to stay close to the king and princess should there be any trouble along the way to the pond."

Hmmm. Little brother once again had shown he was growing up fast and becoming a wise faeryman. Before long, he'd not need his older sibling to watch over him.

Stancian joined Lylan and Jaden. "I'm the obvious choice to take up the rear, being trained as a guard."

Lylan nodded.

As Stancian fell behind, Lylan whispered to Jaden. "If you sense anything unusual, tap my shoulder. Don't say a word."

"Right. My thought exactly." Jaden gave his brother a subtle thumbs-up.

They trudged on through the forest without incident, Lylan dreading the moment his company was no longer needed. As he followed her, he drank in every detail of Princess Jillian to store in his memory. Would he ever again meet anyone who stirred his heart the way this faerylet had? He doubted it.

A couple of hours later, as they were about to turn onto the path that led around the pond, sounds came to Lylan's ears from the darkened woods. Jaden tapped his brother's shoulder. Lylan slipped his hand over Jillian's mouth and pulled her to the ground. "Shhh."

Jaden tugged King Farmeran to the grass and then latched onto the shadair's robe to pull him behind the bushes that surrounded them.

As the guards dragged the gagged detainees into the undergrowth, Lylan surveyed the area to make sure the thick brush concealed everyone. As whatever made the thrashing passed them, would the king's party remain undetected? Lylan peeked through a section of the thicket into the forest.

Shiny metal flashed between the trees. A troop of faerymen guards in royal purple tramped toward Glistineare. *Our family.* Should he continue with the king and princess or follow the band of six guards who had stepped into the open and taken the path that led home?

Lylan glanced at his brother. As Jaden beheld the troop, he pressed his lips together. His eyes narrowed. Lylan touched Jaden's wrist and held up one finger. *Wait.*

He peered over Jillian to address the king and Shadair. Barely above a whisper, Lylan said, "Your Majesty, you, Shadair Vanderrissian, Stancian, and the guards will have to protect Princess Jillian while we handle these thugs. We can't allow our family, or the others in our town, to be harmed."

The king, Stancian, and the shadair nodded their agreement.

Lylan nudged Jaden to backtrack along the path from whence they'd come. Lylan spoke in his brother's ear. "We'll make for the rock gateway that leads to our town and confront them. It will give us the advantage of surprise on higher ground."

Jaden nodded and led the way.

Several minutes later, they reached the stone entryway and took positions behind the largest boulder. As the purple-clad troop approached, Lylan stepped into the passageway. "*Halt!* You've no business here. Drop your swords and retreat." Lylan held his sword in a high position, ready to fight.

The leader of the troop laughed. "And just who do you think you are, scum? You aspire to take on six of the king's guards by yourself?" They spread out to engage.

"Maybe not, but I'm not alone."

Jaden jumped out behind them, two long knives held in his hands. The blades glinted as shafts of sunlight streamed through the forest canopy.

Wings in a flurry, steel clashed against steel. Like a hornet, Jaden stuck in his jabs. He twisted and turned. Distinct glimpses of his powder blue appeared everywhere.

Lylan, as nimble on his feet as his younger brother, leaped into the air to avoid his attackers. He somersaulted and flicked past their thrusts and slashes. He feared he and his brother would tire before they stopped the trespassers.

A flash of white light filled the area. Lylan ducked behind a boulder, Jaden beside him.

As the glare dissipated, the guards dropped their swords at the sight of Shadair Vanderrissian, King Farmeran, Princess Jillian, and Stancian, weapons in hand in a circle around the traitors. A grin spread across Lylan's face.

Stancian cackled. "You didn't think I'd let you have all the fun, did you?"

Lylan laughed. He gazed at the group, each with their weapon pointed at the prince's guards. When his eyes landed on the princess, his mouth dropped open. "Princess Jillian?"

"I've been skilled in the art of swordsmanship since I was a faeryling. My athair made certain I could protect myself." She held her head high.

"Where are the previously captive guards?" Jaden stared wide-eyed at the shadair.

"Not to worry, my boy. They've lost their memories for the time being and sit in wait for our return." He chuckled. "Spells can be very useful at times, as you'll someday find out."

The prince's guards were bound and linked together to walk in single file to join the rest of the captives.

Before the group resumed their journey around the lake, Shadair Vanderrissian faced the guards. "I wouldn't attempt to take any liberties if I were you. You've no idea what powers a shadair possesses."

Lylan and Jaden glanced at each other and pressed their lips tight. Lylan sighed. At least he'd have many things to learn while he tried to forget the love in his heart for Princess Jillian.

Chapter Twenty-One

The procession began the trek around the pond. Princess Jillian fell into step with Lylan. "You were brave to take on the prince's trained guards twice." She smiled. Exactly the kind of faeryman she'd always dreamed would sweep her off her feet. And he had. But he'd go home after the king reclaims his throne.

"And you are quite the extraordinary princess, if you don't mind my saying so." His gaze found hers, and she couldn't turn away. "I admire strong females. My máthair always fought right next to Athair when our town was under attack. We never suspected the attackers came from your village until my athair explained everything the other day."

Jillian stumbled over a rock in the path. Lylan caught her before she fell and wrapped his arms around her. With a snicker, Jaden and Stancian stepped around the two. Heat rushed into Jillian's face and spread to her wings, giving them a pale pink glow.

Lylan straightened and released her.

"Thank you, kind sir." She pretended to straighten her gown. Did he *have* to let go so soon?

"My pleasure."

Each spoke the other's name at the same time.

He grinned at her. "I'm sorry. Go ahead."

"I... well... I wish you'd stay in Amythaseah for a while." *Forever.* She lowered her gaze to the path.

"I suppose I could visit for a little while." He gave her a puzzled stare.

Suddenly, Shadair Vanderrissian stood before them. "Do you think *I* needed another bodyguard for this little walk in the woods? That wasn't why I brought you along, Lylan. You two need to bring things out in the open and stop pussyfooting around. Boy, tell her what's in your heart. And Princess Jillian, no law states royalty and descendants of shadairs cannot have a relationship. I'll not say more, but don't make me have to." With that, he chuckled and vanished.

Jillian and Lylan gaped at each other.

"I will tarry for a while. I want to learn more about you, Princess Jillian."

"Please drop the *princess* part. Call me Jillian. I want to become better acquainted with you as well." Where had Shadair Vanderrissian come from, and where had he gone?

Dylan took her hand. "Let's catch up to the group before we're left behind."

Chapter Twenty-Two

As the royal entourage entered Amythaseah, the inhabitants gawked but then bowed to the king. Lylan's anxious heart warmed at the reception. They remembered their king, though a hundred years had passed.

"King Farmeran, you're alive." An old female faery with ragged wings and clothing stepped forward and bowed before him. "We'd given up hope."

"*Marcel.* Is that you?" She fell on her knees before him. "Why are you not in the palace taking care of my daughter, Fabreena?"

Her head bowed lower, and tears trickled down her face. "Prince Maricent said my services were no longer needed. He sent the princess away. I know not where."

Lylan could almost visualize the steam coming from the king's ears as the muscles in Farmeran's jaw bulged.

"We shall see about that." The king helped the faerywoman to her feet. "Come with me, my good lady."

Marcel fell into line with the rest of the group as several well-dressed citizens fled around the corner of a building. Lylan shook his head. Gone to warn the prince his athair had returned and was none too happy, he assumed.

Reaching the outer gates of the palace grounds had been no trouble. But as soon as the entrance came into view, Lylan counted eight guards before it, swords drawn. "Here we go again." He braced himself to engage in another battle.

Chapter Twenty-Three

Everyone stood still for what seemed an eternity. Lylan didn't let down his guard. He glanced at the shadair. "Why are they standing as if frozen? What are they staring at?"

Shadair Vanderrissian smiled at him. He thrust his fisted hand, thumb out, over his shoulder. The royal entourage turned.

Lylan's brows rose. The entire village must have come out to join the king in the palace takeover, except for the elite, who had wandered off when King Farmeran first appeared. Each resident held an object to use as a weapon. Even the older faerylings had come to support their king.

"Why are we waiting?" Lylan spun to face the shadair.

"Patience. You are a warrior at heart, my boy, but there's no need to engage in battle when the deck of cards is stacked against the enemy." He swung his robed arm toward the gate. Behind the eight guards approached six royal guards.

The guards loyal to Prince Maricent dropped their swords. The royal guards gathered the weapons and bound the eight traitors to the iron gate.

King Farmeran proceeded onto the palace grounds. But as he did, an older faerywoman stepped out of a shop just outside the gate, gasped, and fainted. Lylan rushed to her side and caught her. He eased her to the ground. The king stopped.

"*Máthair?*" Jillian kneeled by her and lifted her parent's limp hand. "Máthair, please wake up. I'm home."

Jillian's máthair blinked and then smiled. "I'd thought I'd lost you forever, like your athair. Prince Maricent removed me from the palace when you left. I've tried to find work, but there's nothing I'm skilled to do."

"We haven't lost Athair. I'll explain later." She and Lylan helped her máthair to her feet. "Everything will be all right. Are you okay?"

Her máthair nodded.

"Let us proceed," the king ordered.

Followed by the shadair and the rest of his group, including the citizens and royal guards who had swelled to number twelve, King Farmeran advanced to the palace. Once everyone entered the grounds, the king stopped and turned. "Please allow me to handle this in my way. Guards, follow me."

As Farmeran ascended the elegant curved stairway to the top, Lylan sensed grief in the king. The guards who stood outside the throne room bowed to King Farmeran before they opened the double doors with a loud whoosh. Farmeran entered with his royal guards. The heavy wooden doors shut.

"Now what?" Lylan studied his great-great grandathair Shadair Vanderrissian.

"Now we wait."

Lylan sighed. He gazed at the village's occupants, most dressed in shabby clothing. How could the prince do this to his people?

Two figures stepped out of a stone doorway at the side of the huge stairway. Jillian gasped. Her hand flew to her mouth. "*Athair!*" She and her máthair ran to the first man who was attired in nothing more than rags. He opened his arms to them.

The second faeryman stepped around them and smiled at Lylan and Jaden. "My boys. My dear grandsons."

"*Grandathair!*" The brothers rushed to him.

Shadair Vanderrissian neared the faerymen. "I'm glad to see you again, Estallan. You, too, *Lord* Raynar. This has been a long time coming, but everything has turned out for the best."

As they spoke, a smaller figure in a soiled gown emerged from the stone doorway. Raynar and Estallan held their hands out to her, and she stepped forward. Marcel flew to Princess Fabreena's side and hugged her, tears streaming down her cheeks. The young faerylet returned her embrace. "I've missed you, Marcel."

Vanderrissian's wings darkened. "Your brother locked you away, did he? He will rue the day." The shadair held out his hand. His wings changed to their brilliant turquoise color. "Come. Your athair is home again."

Princess Fabreena took his hand. "Lord Raynar and Shadair Estallan have taken excellent care of me. They should be rewarded."

"They shall be, my dear."

Lylan grinned. To breathe free air again would be reward enough. *What did his great-great-grandathair have in mind?*

Lord Raynar wrapped his arm around his daughter's waist and held his hand out to shake Vanderrissian's. "Estallan filled me in on your plan. Where is King Farmeran?"

"He's attending to the final details in this affair. The guards who followed Maricent and tried to kill the king will be imprisoned to pay for their crimes against the crown. They will also work to clean up and rebuild the village that has gone to ruin because of the prince's greed."

Lylan's brows lowered. But what of Prince Maricent's treasonous acts? Would he go unpunished? *Because he's a prince?*

Chapter Twenty-Four

few nights later, a huge feast for the entire village was proclaimed. A night of merriment throughout Glorianderis was expected as news of the king's return went out to all the provinces. Peace flooded Lylan's heart.

Lylan and Jaden welcomed their athair, máthair, and sisters into the palace. After introducing them to the king's court, Lylan turned to his brother. "Prince Maricent will pay for the treachery to his athair and people. Though it pained him, King Farmeran has stripped his son of title and wealth. The king has proclaimed Maricent reduced to a commoner. He's to join his *loyal* guards in the work to restore Amythaseah to its former glory."

Jaden grinned as he jabbed his big brother with an elbow and tipped his head toward Stancian. "He's been showing Daleah particular attention since she arrived, and our little sister is aglow."

"Don't you dare tease her," Lylan warned. "I think Stancian is perfect for her." Lylan's heart twinged.

He turned to find Jaden's eyes riveted on Jillian's best friend, Tally. Another perfect pair.

Despite the joy around him, Lylan's heart sank at the thought of his departure tomorrow. Would he ever see Jillian again? Maybe it was only a wishful dream that his great-great-grandathair said he and the princess could have a relationship.

King Farmeran strode into the room with Princess Fabreena on his arm. The music stopped, and the congregation bowed. He ascended the steps to the dais and turned. The princess took her place next to him. "After long deliberation and counsel from Shadair Vanderrissian, I have an announcement to make. It has been brought to my attention that *Lord* Raynar is in truth the late King Andreager's brother and, therefore, is the rightful heir to our kingdom."

Gasps rose through the ballroom.

Prince Raynar left his wife and daughter and approached the throne. At the stairs, he bowed. His eyes met the king's. "I've been content to be your advisor, Your Majesty, and as such I desire to remain, if it be your will. I vow my allegiance to King Farmeran, who the people have declared a just and honest ruler. I agree."

Farmeran descended the stairs and threw his arms around Raynar. "You shall be my best and only advisor, outside of the shadairs, and also my brother instead of an uncle. You are no longer *Lord* Raynar, but *Prince* Raynar."

Well, that settles that. Lylan's chin sank to his chest. As if she weren't already far enough above him. She'd pick a prince to wed for sure. Many would seek the hand of such a fair princess.

King Farmeran whispered to Prince Raynar as they sat on dual thrones before the crowd at the feast. The prince nodded to the king and grinned. Raynar stood. The room became as quiet as a cave.

"His Royal Majesty reminded me of a long-standing law regarding the status of a princess when she comes of age. She must choose a prince for her husband. My Jillian has come of age." He turned to his daughter, who sat at the end of a long table.

Jillian's jaw dropped. "But, Athair... I... we... don't know any prince except the king's son, and his title has been taken away." She let out an audible sigh.

Lylan breathed a burst of air between his lips. Good thing too. He'd be switched if he'd allow her to fall into the miscreant's hands. What would they do? Postpone the event until a prince from another kingdom was found?

King Farmeran stood. "I proclaim an old law reinstated. Shadairs were once given the title of prince by reason of their exceptional skills and talents. As of today, Shadair Vanderrissian will be known as Shadair Prince Vanderrissian, which makes his great-great-grandson, Lylan, who has now fully inherited his powers... Shadair Prince Lylan. Please stand."

As Lylan stood, cheers resounded around him. He was led to the dais where he joined his grandathair Shadair Prince Estallan and great-great grandathair Shadair Prince Vanderrissian. The king placed a golden crown studded with crystals to match their wings on each of the three shadairs' heads.

After the king read and signed the decrees, Prince Raynar flew to his daughter's side and took her hand. He raised her from her chair and brought her to Lylan's side. "I choose Shadair Prince Lylan to wed my fair daughter, Princess Jillian."

Lylan's eyes widened. This had to be a dream. That was it. He'd awake at home in his bed. Prince Raynar closed Lylan's open mouth with his index finger.

Jillian's eyes filled with tears. Lylan's heart sank again. She must be in love with someone in the village. Of course, she would be. *I can't let this happen to her. It isn't fair.* His brows crumpled. "I'm honored, Prince Raynar, but I fear your daughter's heart is already taken. Cannot something be done to change the law?"

She gazed up at Lylan and swiped away the tears with her hands. "Yes, my heart was captured the first time you helped me when I fell in the woods. My heart belongs to you, Lylan. And it always will. I love you, but do you love me?"

In less than a second, Lylan answered her question with a kiss that lifted them off the ground and spun them round and round like a dandelion seed puffball on a breeze.

Cheers erupted, and fireworks filled the air.

As the thrill of the moment subsided, and the couple landed on their feet in the ballroom, Lylan drew Jillian into another warm embrace and touched her lips with his. As their kiss deepened, her wings sparkled in a rainbow of colors, and the village of Amythaseah glowed with a brighter, purer amethyst light, signaling a new era in the world of Glorianderis.

The End

Postscript: And they lived happily ever after.

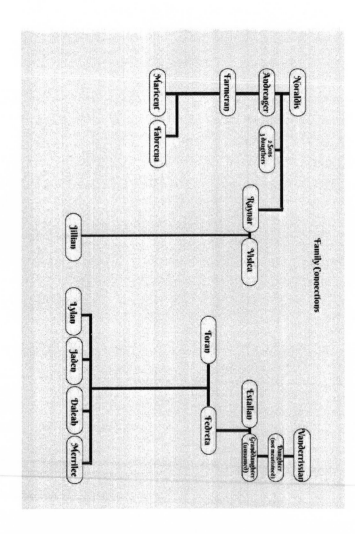

About the Author

Sharon K Connell writes stories about people who discover God will allow things in their lives to bring them to a saving knowledge of Jesus Christ and/or increase their faith. Her genre is Christian romance suspense, always with a dose of humor and very often a mystery. She has also written short stories in other genres.

Although born in Wisconsin, Sharon was raised in Illinois and went to school through college in Chicago. She has also lived in Missouri, California, Florida, and Ohio. Her travels have taken her to all but six states in the United States, and she has visited Canada and Mexico. She is now a resident of Texas.

Sharon is a member of the American Christian Fiction Writers organization, Houston Writers Guild, CyFair Writers, and the Christian Womens Writers Club (CWW). She runs the Facebook group forum called Christian Writers & Readers and puts out Novel Thoughts, a monthly newsletter for writers as well as readers. Sharon is also a contributing author of inspirational articles for the global online magazine *Faith on Every Corner*.

She is a graduate of the Pensacola Bible Institute in Florida and holds a certificate in fiction writing from the International Writing Program through the University of Iowa.

Let the words of my mouth, and the meditation of my heart, be acceptable in thy sight, O Lord, my strength, and my redeemer.
Psalm 19:14

Links

Website: www.authorsharonkconnell.com
Amazon Author Page: http://www.amazon.com/author/sharonkconnell
Author's book page on Facebook:
https://www.facebook.com/averypresenthelpbook1
Author's Page on Facebook:
https://www.facebook.com/ChristianRomanceSuspense/
Group Forum on Facebook:
https://www.facebook.com/groups/ChristianWritersAndReadersGroup
Forum/
Twitter: https://twitter.com/SharonKConnell
Goodreads: https://www.goodreads.com/SharonKConnell
LinkedIn: https://www.linkedin.com/in/sharonkconnell
Pinterest: https://www.pinterest.com/rosecastle1/

Other Works

Novels
A Very Present Help
Paths of Righteousness
There Abideth Hope
His Perfect Love
Treasure in a Field
Ko'olau's Secret
Tall Pines Sanctuary

Novella
Icicles to Moonbeams ~ Christmas Eve Blessings

Short Story Collection
Sharon's Shorts ~ A Multi-Genre Collection of Short Stories

Short Stories in Anthologies
"Ding-A-Ling Holiday Blues"
In *Tales of Texas, Vol. 2*

"Spirit Lake"
In *Dark Visions*

Thank you for reading.

Made in the USA
Middletown, DE
20 November 2022

14989293R00073